Fated Summer

A
Hybrid Home
Paranormal Romance Story

By

JOSETTE REUEL

Fated Summer: Hybrid Home 1
Copyright c) 2017 Josette Reuel
Cover design by Evanlea Publishing Services
Photo contributor: BIGSTOCKphoto.com and
www.Canva.com
Proofreading and edits: Evanlea Publishing Services and
Reuel's Rebels' Beta Crew.

ISBN-13: 978-1986487634
ISBN-10: 1986487636

Zinnia Boushay is at a crossroads in her life. After being laid off from her long-time job, she decided that a summer adventure is just what she needs to determine her direction. Up to this point, she'd only been going through the motions and she's now ready to make some long-term choices. However, running into a beast on the beach wasn't quite what she expected.

Zvar Noir traveled the world trying to find answers to how he could end his own torment. Time was running out and he once again traveled to the North Carolina beach where he had been abandoned all of those years ago. The beast inside of him was once again rising and he wasn't sure if he had the strength to keep fighting the inevitable. His mentor had taught him many things, most of all what he was, but to Zvar he'd always be a monster. Nothing was going to change that, so maybe now was the time to admit defeat.

However, Fate always has her plans laid well in advance and Zinnia's spur of the moment vacation might just be what leads Zvar to find his strength.

— * —

A summer vacation to decide her future leads Zinnia to find her worst fear... or is the monster her deepest desire?

Dedication

To lazy summer days with the ones you love.

Acknowledgments

Every book is possible in large part to the support of my family. I learned to use my imagination at a young age thanks to the encouragement of my parents. And, I'm able to write romance because I had some of the best instructors — thanks mom, dad, and Chris (my husband). Of course, I wouldn't be the woman I am without my children — they support me and bring joy to my heart.

As always, I send my gratitude out to all of those on Facebook — authors, readers, family, and friends (*those I've met, those I hope to meet one day*) — for words of wisdom, for words of joy, and for sharing pieces of your lives with me.

To my Beta readers... your input is priceless. And, a special thank you to all the fans — your support and promotion of my work are invaluable. Beta Readers for this book: Jennifer Miranda Alvarez, Birgit Wahl, Alison Jarvis, and Melanie Nikendei.

Lastly, a special thank you to my PAs — *Jennifer Rebelle Alvarez* and *Siobhan Isaac* — who inspire me, keep me focused and remind me to not overdo it. Destiny brought us together and I couldn't be more grateful for finding friends like you.

Chapter 1

*Z*innia stared off into the sunset, her toes curling into the still warm sand of the North Carolina beach. Relaxing, she breathed in the salty sea air. Vacation. It had been over five years since she'd last taken time off from work. So, when she was laid off from her job, she took it as fate's way of telling her to go on an adventure.

She'd taken the nudge to heart and packed her tiny car. With the loss of her job, she'd sold everything she could, donated a bunch, and packed all of her remaining belongings into her little beat up Ford Fiesta. Nothing held her where she was — her parents moved to Florida the year before — and her friends were more work acquaintances if she was being honest. She could get sad over her lonely life or say, Fuck It, and enjoy the opportunity she now had.

No strings. No responsibilities.

Zinnia was more than ready to have an adventure.

Originally, she'd thought about driving down to visit her parents, but after a few hours on the road, she realized going *home* was not the adventurous thing to do. Instead, she took a random exit from the highway she'd been driving. From that point on, she took random turns until she saw the signs for the coast.

Hours later she still had no idea where her final stop would be, but she was grateful to have everything she owned in the car with her. It made it much easier… she had pretty much anything she would need no matter where the wind took her.

The long drive gave her plenty of time to look back over her life and ponder what she wanted her next steps to be. Granted, she was no closer to the epiphany she'd hoped for, but eighteen hours later, she was extremely grateful that her meandering road trip ended at the ocean. Zinnia always loved the water and spending at least a week doing nothing but sitting on the beach sounded like the perfect summer vacation. If she was lucky, she'd find a man with whom she could have the cliché summer fling, too.

A yawn cracked her jaw, a clear sign it was way past time for her to find a place to lodge for the night. She hadn't been searching for a place to bed down or even paying attention to where she was when she stopped. Hell, she'd stopped in a town so small that an ill-timed blink had almost caused her to miss it.

Zinnia chuckled as she turned to walk back up the beach. Following her footsteps, she searched the darkening twilight for the trail that had led her to the shoreline from the road. Another yawn caused her to stumble over a bump in the sand. Obviously, she was exhausted. The truth was, the blink, which caused her to almost miss the pull off for the beach just outside of Rodanthe, North Carolina, had been her eyes closing due to fatigue. She definitely needed sleep. She might even take a nap in the car before getting back on the road to search for a hotel. With some rest, everything would be clearer.

As the sun set, darkness inched along the sand, causing the seagrass to cast long waving shadows. A slight breeze came off the water making Zinnia shiver and wrap her arms tightly around herself. It might be summer, but the encroaching night held the beginnings of autumn — which was a short six weeks away. This trip would be one last free-for-all over the remaining summer days before she decided what to do with her life. She gave herself a deadline of the first of September if she hadn't made a definite decision she would head to her parents. Until then, fun was on the menu.

A snapping sound off to Zinnia's right caused her head to jerk in the direction from where it came. Her footsteps stumbled as her eyes roamed over the foliage and stones littering the distance, which still separated her from the road. Her vision swam due to the constantly shifting shadows and her fatigue. The path in front of her was now completely covered in blurry black and gray.

With the cooling night and the deepening darkness, Zinnia couldn't help but wonder at her own stupidity. She shouldn't have stopped here. A woman alone in the dark... it was a horror movie come to life. Clasping her arms even tighter around her body, Zinnia's fear pushed her to more closely examine her immediate surroundings. Shadows took on menacing shapes until her scrutiny proved them to be a bush or large rock. A weak chuckle escaped as she realized it was better to get back to the car quickly than stand out here like a horror movie bimbette.

Once again turning forward, Zinnia quickened her steps only to be stopped short after a few feet.

A large shadow rose from the walkway, blocking Zinnia's path. The hulking form of a man took shape in the darkness. Her breath caught in her throat as she struggled to scream. Fear swamped her. Zinnia wanted to run but was rooted in place.

Every scary movie she'd ever been forced to watch came back to life in her mind. *Fuck me*, her inner-voice whimpered. Maybe she was a horror movie bimbette.

Zinnia watched as a large hand reached toward her and her scream finally broke free. The release of sound unfroze her, she spun on her feet just to become tangled in something she couldn't see. Another scream stabbed into the night as darkness loomed up behind her eyelids.

He was starving. The small town where he resided would notice if anyone went missing, but he needed to eat, and it wouldn't be smart to deny himself too much longer.

He'd been walking along the beach-side road when an enticing scent of a warm-blooded female caught his attention. Her appetizing aroma drew him to her like a moth to a flame.

At first, he fought the allure of her that came to him on the breeze. Reminding himself once again about not wanting to become a science experiment didn't have its usual impact. Desperately needing a distraction he pulled out all the stops and began listing all of his belongings — alphabetically — in his mind. It was a feeble attempt, between his old hunger and a new one now burning down his spine to his groin, there was no way he could control the monster inside.

The beast wanted her. Nothing would keep it from its prey.

The shackles that had been thinning over the past several days snapped. He ghosted down the path in search of his prey. As he roamed closer, her scent became stronger. With each step, he began to make out the subtle nuances — warm, sweet, and woodsy with lavender and vanilla. She drew him like no other.

He yearned to see her, to hold her, to taste her.

So, when he finally came upon the woman, he couldn't stop himself from reaching out to her.

Her screams ripped through him, slashing at his heart. Stumbling at the effect she had on him he almost missed her reaction to his beastly appearance.

It was as if he watched her move in slow motion, her feet tangled in a bunch of vegetation, she teetered as if waiting for gravity to decide. Her body twisted in an odd direction and he noted her eyes falling closed as she began a descent to the ground. However, she never made it to the hard-packed sand, he was at her side in a breath with his arms wrapped solidly around her before she could fall more than a few inches.

As she nestled into his arms, the contact mentally knocked him on his ass from the realizations caused by her nearness. The beast roared, flexing its muscles against the mental cage that contained it. But, it was no use. The truth about the woman in his arms was all it took to shut all of his baser desires down.

Swinging her up into his arms he turned to the road heading to his home. When she snuggled into his neck, the vibrations she caused in his body punctuated what finding this woman tonight meant for him... *she was his.*

Chapter 2

Zvar sat in a chair beside the bed watching the woman sleep. Classically beautiful, her short hair curled slightly where it fanned out on the sheets. The darkness of it framed her oval face, bringing out the olive tones in her skin — skin all rosy-hued with vitality and life.

The beast stirred. Zvar tightened the grip on the mental leash with which he had it contained.

His stomach grumbled at his lack of nourishment. Another night with no food, but he couldn't bring himself to care. He gazed at the female as he shoved his own needs to the side and continued to wait for her to awake.

Zvar would wait for her no matter how long it took — this woman was *everything*.

Once the female was conscious, he could claim her. The single thought echoed in his mind, circling itself over and over. He'd claim her and she'd provide the nourishment he needed of her own free will. If his mentor was correct, his mate could feed him with no ill effects. He would no longer need to steal life... it would be freely given.

But, what if Clyde was wrong? His gaze zeroed in on the rising fall of the woman's chest. He made out the strong beat of her heart — could he take the chance of silencing the drumbeat of his own soul?

Mentally ticking off the possibilities, he realized things might not be as cut and dry as he had hoped. All he knew... the female was *his*. Even so, he wouldn't force her into his way of life. Her scent gave her away — his woman was one hundred percent human. Not to mention her reaction to him on the beach. From the reaction, he was guessing she knew nothing of the things hiding in the shadows. Things like himself.

All of his base needs would be ignored for her happiness. He would do anything to ensure her happiness. He recognized it as certainly as he knew he was a monster thanks to his sperm donor's DNA. But, Zvar would end his own miserable life before he hurt the woman sleeping peacefully in his bed.

Morning light broke through a crack between the heavy curtains at the window. As time ticked by, Zvar followed the misty beam of light as it inched closer to the bed. His vision was sharp enough to pick up the dust motes dancing in the beam from where he sat in the shadows. He seldom went out during the day, only if it was absolutely necessary. The shadows and muted light of the latter part of the day were more to his liking. However, watching the beam finally reach his female, as it set the reddish tints in her hair to flame and caused her silky skin to glow, he reevaluated the joy to be had during the day. Why would he want to deny himself the beauty of his mate in the sun?

Zvar's eyelids grew heavy. A lack of sleep and sustenance both causing his energy to flag... he soon drifted off to sleep.

Zinnia slowly came to consciousness. She was groggy with sleep, so she snuggled down into the soft mattress and the warm comforter of her bed. Her mind drifted in that foggy half-dream state just before you wake. However, as she fought off wakefulness, dark images rose in her mind. Shadows moving across the sand, rising to form a man... no, a monster. It reached for her...

Zinnia bolted up in the bed. She covered her mouth with her hand to muffle her panting breaths as she surveyed her unfamiliar surroundings.

Stretching her senses she could hear waves crashing against the shoreline. Dropping her hands to the bed, she ran her fingers over the silky-soft material of the high-quality bedding. *Did I make it to a hotel last night?* she wondered as she considered the room surrounding her.

The window provided plenty of hazy sunlight, allowing her to scan every surface for some sign of how she ended up in the room. She took in rich furnishings and expensive decorations — there was no way she could afford a hotel like this. *How did I end up in this room?* she continued to ask herself.

Minutes ticked by with no answers until her gaze fell on a chair in the shadows, then the night before came slamming into her with one hundred percent clarity. *A monster.*

The scream broke free from her throat before she could choke it down. She gawked in horror as the man... no monster... jumped from the chair. He was huge compared to her — his broad shoulders large enough to block her view of anything past the bed as he took an attack stance in front of her. She observed scales slithering over the tan skin of his bare back, giving it an opalescent hue wherever the scales appeared. His hair lengthened, turning an icy-blue color as it curled around his shoulders.

Zinnia watched in terrified fascination as he turned in her direction, his eyes glowed with an inner fire and his nostrils flared as he inhaled.

Scrambling backward on the bed, Zinnia clutched at the comforter as if it was made of steel and could protect her from the creature in front of her. She plastered her back to the headboard and the engraved wood pressed into her flesh through her t-shirt.

Glancing around she sensed the monster relax as he stood up tall. His fists fell to his sides. He closed his eyes as he breathed in and out through his mouth several times.

Zinnia's heart continued to pound in her chest, but her fear backed off enough to allow her mind to begin thinking of escape.

"There is no danger, female." The deep voice vibrated through her, sending heat surging into parts of her that shouldn't be reacting in her current circumstance.

She noticed the scales begin to recede. Shock coursed through her as the hair turned dark brown and shrunk until it laid in a stylish short haircut. When the man finally turned his gaze to her once again, they no longer glowed but shown a vibrant, but normal, hazel green.

"You are safe."

"Wh..." Her words came out as a croak, forcing her to swallow while trying to find her voice. "Where am I?"

"Home."

"It's not my..." she stammered as his gaze took her in.

Zinnia lost her train of thought as she sank into his beautiful eyes.

"You're home," he reiterated and pulled her back to the conversation.

"Why?"

"Why not?"

Zinnia couldn't hold back her huff of aggravation. She'd never been one to cower — living alone since she was eighteen, she dealt with her own needs and learned to be aware of danger and how to avoid it. On the few occasions when she couldn't, she'd stood up for herself and this time would be no different. It wasn't smart to appear weak.

She could have avoided this confrontation if only she'd paid attention last night to the approaching darkness. It was her own stupidity that had put her in this situation.

Irritation at herself added more edge to her voice when she spoke again.

"Now, see here, I don't know you and this is not my home. I just need you to move. I need to gather myself, then leave. Okay? Okay." Clinging to her false bravado, Zinnia moved to the edge of the large bed.

"No." The man... creature... monster... whatever he was, stood taller at the end of the bed with his arms crossed.

The change caught Zinnia's gaze. She couldn't help but follow the movement of the muscles flexing along those strong arms and over the muscular chest. Absently, she licked her lips as she stopped midway between getting up from the mattress.

A glow lit up the man's eyes as they both stood there staring each other down.

"No offense, but you can't keep me here."

"I can."

Zinnia thanked her lucky stars for his short answers because with each word she felt herself wanting to drop to her knees and worship the ground he walked on. It made her hackles rise... her anger pushing back the fog the voice created in her brain. She dropped the blanket she still clung to and stormed over to within a foot of the hard, muscled body.

Again she caught herself licking her lips as she tried to fight back the fire starting to run through her veins. With each degree her temperature rose, anger followed until it blocked out her fear.

"Now, you see here..." She poked her finger into his chest just above his arms. "I am not your prisoner. I will be leaving."

A sexy as sin smile spread across his lips as one arm dropped to his side while his other hand caressed her cheek. Zinnia wanted to fight the feelings overwhelming her, but she found herself staring into the face of the man of her dreams.

"My sweet one, you have such fire, such strength." His words dripped over her like warm honey. "Let me take care of you... feed you..."

Of its own accord, her head nodded yes and allowed him to take her hand. He lay a soft kiss on her palm before leading her from the room.

Chapter 3

Zvar recognized that his cursed voice was soothing his mate and allowing him to coax her into doing what he wanted. Well, not entirely true, what he wanted was to take her back to his bed — the beast agreed... *take her, devour her,* it whispered.

He reminded himself of his vows to himself. He would allow her to choose.

Against his own desires, he led her to the kitchen and once she took a seat, he cooked a simple breakfast of eggs, bacon, and toast.

"Here you are, my sweet. Would you like some orange juice?"

"Yes, thank you."

She began to nibble on the food he'd prepared for her. Her movements were dainty, causing worry to settle into him. Her seeming fragility causing concern to settle into his mind... fear he might hurt her or break her. But, a soothing sense of pride also filled him. A pride from his ability to provide for her, feed her, and care for her.

"Do you need anything else?" he asked.

"Thank you, but no. This is good." She motioned to her half-empty plate.

He smiled as they sat in silence for a few minutes. Zvar inhaled her sweet and earthy scent which caused the beast to squirm in his gut. He gripped the edge of his seat, struggling to keep his agitation invisible to the woman sitting across from him at the table.

In a need to distract himself further, Zvar decided to learn more about his mate.

"Well, now that you are awake and fed...." He grinned. "You passed out on the beach. You didn't have any identification, I didn't know who you were or where you lived, so I brought you here to my home."

Worry shown in the line of her mouth and the crinkled corners of her slightly squinted eyes as she took him in. She absently dropped her fork back to the plate before answering.

"I'm Zinnia Boushay," she finally responded. "I remember shadows and a... a..."

Zinnia. He liked the name. Hearing it had him picturing the flower of the same name — delicate petals and vibrant colors — beautiful. Put simply, she was breathtaking. The more he examined her, the more he picked up. She was strong, but not in a go-to-the-gym-everyday sort of way. She was intelligent — he almost caught the motion of her mind whirling behind her eyes as she stumbled over her words. He couldn't wait to find out more.

"I'm not sure what I saw." Zinnia shook her head as if to clear it. "Then, in the bedroom... What are you?"

"I'm Zvar," he replied.

It wasn't far from the truth. His name meant *beast* — he wouldn't deny he was a monster with little more than animal instinct guiding him most days. But, he didn't want to admit it to her yet. Zvar didn't want her to fear him and right now... right now, he smelled weariness and curiosity coming off of her skin. Those feelings he could work with.

She cocked her head to the side as she peered at him.

"What is a Zvar?"

"Not what... who. I'm Zvar."

"Okay, Zvar." Zinnia straightened in her chair while staring into his eyes. "What are you, Zvar?"

"What are you, Zinnia Boushay?" He cocked his head, waiting for her response.

"I'm one hundred percent human, but I don't believe you are? It doesn't make sense, but I remember what I saw... it's not the man you're showing me at this moment. What I saw was... more than human."

Zvar sighed. His mate was intelligent and had retained her memories against his hopes. He would have to tell her the truth.

"Your eyes literally glow, Zvar. I also remember what appeared to be... scales... and your hair changed."

"Yes," he answered wearily before taking a breath to answer her real question. "I'm not *human*, but *you* don't need to be afraid of me. All I want is to care for you."

Zinnia wore a confused expression. He watched her fingers as they fidgeted with her long-forgotten fork.

"So many questions," she mumbled under her breath, but he had no difficulty picking up her words.

Taking a deep breath, he decided to open up to his mate. She was the only living creature he would ever want to tell everything, share everything, and give everything. He pushed down his barriers, allowing his beast to rise.

✦

Zinnia's breath caught as he became the *more* that she'd seen.

Oh, my God! I didn't imagine it… he really does have blue hair. Zinnia struggled to gain her composure. She wasn't sure why she wasn't afraid though somewhere deep in her mind she knew she should be — she was prey and he was the predator. However, instead of searching for the nearest exit, her body ignited with lust and her mind filled with questions. Not only was Zvar gorgeous, he was intriguing, too. His answers were always clipped short, which made her want to pull more from him.

In the bedroom, his voice had mesmerized her… no, more than that, it had made her want to do anything he asked her to do. But, as her mind cleared away the fog of sleep, she realized his words didn't so much compel her against her will, as they emotionally pulled her to the man of her own desire. It was a tug down deep inside of her, which made her want to follow him to find out what might happen between them.

Zvar rose from his chair allowing her to see all of him. Standing in front of her in only his jeans, he allowed her time to take in all the subtle differences between this form and his human one.

His bare feet were braced shoulder's width apart as he moved his hands behind his back. The action caused his biceps to bulge, causing her to bite her lip to keep from gasping. Compared to her, Zvar was large. He towered over her average height. The width of his shoulders giving the impression he'd swallow her whole. Even so, as she took a closer inspection, his muscles weren't overly massive — more those of a daily swimmer than a bodybuilder downing protein shakes and lifting twice their body weight. She liked Zvar's build. She really, really liked Zvar's body.

Curiosity took control and had her rising to approach him. At the sound of a growl, her mind finally caught up with her actions, stopping her less than an inch from touching his skin. Her eyes snapped to his face and she noticed his nostrils flare as he inhaled. Another growl escaped. Again, she was hit by her lack of fear. Zvar was a creature from a paranormal novel or fantasy film, yet here he stood in the flesh, and Zinnia knew she should run for the door. But, she couldn't force her feet to move in the direction of safety. Besides, she was pretty sure she didn't want to leave.

"Zvar?"

"Yes," he replied, his voice deeper and darker than it had been.

"Can I touch your scales?" she asked with awe in her voice.

He groaned and nodded his reply.

She lightly caressed her fingers over the scales on his forearm. The parts of his skin without the scales was warm and supple whereas the scales were hard and had a chill to them. The strangeness intrigued her. She couldn't stop moving her fingers along his arm, eventually reaching his chest.

A growl vibrated under her palm and Zinnia gazed up to find Zvar's eyes glowing with the unearthly light from last night and again this morning when she first woke.

"Zinnia, stop," he pleaded. "I only have a limited amount of control over the beast."

Shock shook her. "What beast?"

"Don't be afraid, please. I won't let it hurt you."

"Zvar, what beast?"

"The half of my DNA gifted by my evil Unseelie father," he whispered as his eyelids closed her out.

Memories from movies and books zinged through her mind as she processed the word — Unseelie. Zvar was telling her that not only were the Fae real, but the dark Fae were as well. Could anyone be as bad as Zvar made himself sound?

"Explain." Zinnia had so many questions it seemed simpler to give him the one-word demand than to barrage him with the jumbled mess overtaking her brain.

With a sigh, Zvar gripped her hand in his own. Her fingers disappeared in his grip as he lifted her hand to lay a sweet kiss on her palm.

"Have a seat, my sweet. Just promise me you'll hear me out. Don't run and I'll tell you everything."

Zinnia nodded. Fear was the farthest thing from her mind. All she felt was curiosity and the indescribable pull of this male.

Once they were both seated across from each other back at the kitchen table, Zvar cleared his throat while his gaze soaked her up. He seemed to be waiting for something.

"Please, Zvar, go ahead. I'll stay right here, I promise."

He cleared his throat again before beginning.

"My biological parents abandoned me as an infant. Humans found me and with no family, I ended up in the system. I bounced from one foster care home to another until I turned fourteen. Up to that point, I only have vague memories — or maybe a dream — of a pale man with coal black hair and a beautiful woman with green hair swimming in the ocean with me. The woman was my mother. I knew this because in my dreams I sensed the love she had for the man and me. The man, however, scared me. He was sinister, causing nightmares that had me sitting up in bed sweating and clawing at my own skin.

I never understood why, but the foster families never seemed to accept me. They were always weary and before long they'd send me packing with some story about something I did. I never remembered misbehaving or doing the things they told the councilors. After about the fifth home, I stopped hoping for a real family. Being blamed constantly for someone else's actions caused me to grow withdrawn, which made it even more difficult to connect with the foster parents.

Then, about a month after I turned fourteen, puberty hit and the beast rose within me. That's when I realized I had been doing the things I had been accused of doing. The beast had been taking control of me in my sleep. So, at fourteen I ran away from the current foster home and began searching for answers.

Unfortunately, it took me several years to find someone to teach me how to take control. During those years the blackouts continued, but now they were happening during the day, while I was awake. It didn't take long for me to realize a trail of dead bodies followed behind me. I was a killer. But, even that knowledge didn't dampen my will to live or my need for answers.

Thankfully, when I was twenty-three, I met Clyde. From somewhere in the southern states, Clyde's an alligator shifter who introduced me to the paranormal world. He answered my questions. However, I soon realized I should have stayed in the dark, knowledge wasn't power in this case. Knowing what I'd been born into and that I had to be a killer or die… I was a young man with no real experience, how in the world was I supposed to deal with being a monster?"

Zvar's voice petered out while he dropped his face into his hands where they lay on the table.

"Zvar?" Zinnia cleared her throat. "Zvar, what are you? Explain it to me."

Even now, after he admitted to killing people, Zinnia couldn't bring herself to fear him or leave.

"As I mentioned, my father is an Unseelie Fae. His Unseelie class… well, the easiest way to describe it…"

"Just spit it out, Zvar. Rip the band-aid off, it's always easier just to do it." She reached across the table and gripped one of his hands as he raised his head to look her in the eyes.

"He's an energy vampire, for lack of a better term. He steals the life force of a living organism to keep himself alive. When he met my mother, he had planned to consume her as he had everything else, but he couldn't... she was his destined mate, the one living creature able to feed an energy vampire and survive. So, instead of killing her, he mated her. I was the byproduct of their union. From what I've been able to cobble together, my mother escaped and returned to her home under the sea."

"Under the sea?" Zinnia interrupted.

"Yes, my mother is a mermaid. A rare one, actually… a siren. I not only have the appearance and darkness of my father, but I have the enchanting voice of my mother."

"Wow." Zinnia couldn't keep the awe from her voice.

She had always enjoyed a good paranormal romance and listening to Zvar's story, she easily pictured him walking right off the pages of one of her favorite books. She felt the pain brought on by his story, her heart ached for him, but she couldn't keep the anticipation from building — excitement zapping through her body when he said two words… *destined mate.*

Her brain still fought but her heart already accepted what Zvar was to her. The connection tying them together strengthened with each second they spent together. Zinnia wanted Zvar with all of her being. It was crazy. She was positive her parents would want to lock her up in the loony bin if they knew, but she didn't care. Zvar was the only thing that mattered to her now and she had an overwhelming urge to help him deal with his past.

Chapter 4

So, you're an Unseelie Fae and a siren hybrid? Why does your ancestry make you a monster?"

Zvar studied his woman, wondering if there was something wrong with her. How could a human ask him that question while remaining seated after everything he had told her? He inhaled and the scents of curiosity and lust assaulted him. Was she experiencing the same connection that he was feeling? Essentially, being raised as a human, Zvar himself had a difficult time dealing with the paranormal and he was a card-carrying member. It was common knowledge that humans didn't have a mating bond. Without the ties of the deeper bond, was it even possible for her to sense the vibration that occurred whenever he was near her?

"Zvar?" Her sweet, feminine voice dragged him from his own thoughts.

"You've seen me. How can you ask me that? Especially, after I told you about the way I've had to survive."

"Survive?"

"Yes, I've killed, Zinnia. I've stolen the life force of living beings in order to continue living." Zvar refused to count the number of lives he had ended, but they always surfaced in his dreams. The ghosts always got their pound of flesh as they chased him through his dreams

and out into the real world. Once the spirits of the
murdered caught up to him, he'd move on, hoping a
change of scenery would help control the hunger. But,
nothing ever changed. The beast remained inside of him,
continuing to steal from those not ready to give.

Zvar saw the struggle waged behind Zinnia's eyes.
He waited for the ax to drop and her to run.

"I won't hurt you, Zinnia. You are the one person
I could never hurt."

Her head jerked upward, and she gazed straight
into his eyes. "Why?"

"I'm pretty sure you've figured it out."

Zvar watched her gulp down her initial reaction.
She licked her lips as her gaze stayed locked on his own.

Zinnia bit her lip for several long seconds before
voicing her response.

"Destined mates."

Her voice was barely a whisper, but he heard it
clear as a bell and it hit him like a locomotive... this
woman was his mate. He'd figured it out the night before
on the beach, but having her voice those two words, gave
the situation a whole new level of importance... of reality.
This was his life and his woman.

"I won't pretend to understand any of this, Zvar,
but I know what I feel. It may have only been a few
hours, but the connection is there. I really want to learn
more... to figure out where this might go."

One moment he was listening to her words... the
next he had her swooped up into his arms. Their mouths
crashed together, both of them wanting to learn the taste

and texture of each other's lips. Her hands rested on each side of his face as she nibbled. Soon, she pressed her plush lips along his mouth and jaw. Fire rose within, burning away the beast which consumed him for what seemed an eternity. With this woman in his arms, the beast was no more.

Joy surged as he lifted Zinnia until she wrapped her legs around his waist. Her tongue swiped along his upper lip and Zvar took advantage. He jabbed his tongue deep into her mouth allowing him to truly taste his mate for the first time. She was so sweet. So *his*. Consumed by the fires of lust, he easily carried her down the hallway to his bedroom.

Carefully laying her out on his bed, Zinnia whined as his lips detached and he stood back to take her in. There was just something about having his woman in his bed that made him hard as iron.

Zinnia's hooded eyes followed his hand as he reached down to flip open the button of his jeans. The intensity in her eyes caused him to freeze with his fingers on the tab of his zipper. But only for a few seconds, that's all the patience his lust-fueled thoughts would allow. Not to mention the pain was beginning to register as his dick enlarged and pressed more firmly into the metal teeth of the zipper. *I'm going to need to start wearing underwear,* he thought with a chuckle. There was no way his shaft would survive what this woman did to him without the cotton cloth between the zipper of his jeans and his skin. Underwear shopping had to be added to his to-do list. That thought, however, had him thinking of buying Zinnia some underwear. No... lingerie, women wore flimsy bits of satin and lace that covered so little while completely obstructing a man's view. His woman would be ravishing in red satin. As he pictured her laying on the bed in the lingerie he wanted to purchase for her, the simmering heat blazed to full force, causing waves of molten lava to wash over him.

Zvar ripped the zipper down with the loud clicking of the metal teeth making the tale-tale unzipping sound. Shoving at the waistband of his jeans he pushed the stiff material over his ass and down his legs. Now free, his cock stuck straight out twitching with his movements. His mate's eyes were round in shock as she took him in. He prayed she liked what she saw because he knew he loved what he saw when he looked at her.

Leaning forward, he braced himself on the edge of the bed. All of his weight balanced on one knee as he ran his eyes from her toes to her eyes.

"Are you ready for me, my sweet?" Zinnia's head nodded uncertainly. "We can stop if you're not ready, Zinnia."

With the lust riding him, it might take an act of God, but he would stop himself right now if she asked it of him.

"No." The word was barely a sound as her voice was heavy with lust and breathy with her own need. "I want you Zvar. At first, I was afraid it was something you were doing to me, but now I understand… this is all you and me. I *want* you. I *need* you. It's all my own desire driving me. Please don't leave me like this? My skin is on fire and I feel like I'll die if you don't do something to quench the thirst of the flames."

The need in her voice called to something deep inside of him. He was inching up her body as soon as her last word left her lips. He pressed light kisses along her skin, beginning at the instep of one dainty foot he ran his kisses and his fingers up each leg. As he neared the juncture of her thighs, fear once again entered his mind. His body shook with his need, but Zvar did not want to hurt this woman in any way. *What if the beast takes control?* he wondered as he withdrew from her skin.

Zinnia's fingers twisted into his hair. She tugged at the strands until his gaze rose to lock with her own.

"Don't even think about it... I need you."

The icy blue of his hair reminded him of what he was, waking him from his lust-fueled dream he pulled his head back, but the woman wouldn't release him.

"What is wrong, Zvar?" Lust was waning and concern entered her voice.

Zvar shook his head while glancing away. His eyes landed on the light falling through the crack in his curtains. His mate was pure like that light. Sweet as sugar. Her scent still engulfed him as he fought to cling to his humanity, to do what he knew was right. He didn't deserve this woman.

Flicking his eyes to Zinnia, then away in a flash so fast he knew she wouldn't catch it, he took her in... for the last time, he inhaled her scent and soaked up her beauty. She might be his mate, but he was a monster. A murderer. She deserved better than him.

For the first time, he embraced the powers granted to him by his lineage and flashed himself to the beach. Completely nude, he raced into the surf.

Zvar's body acclimated to the water and the other side of his heritage took control. Gills appeared at his throat while webbing grew between his toes and fingers. Then scales raced along his skin, covering him from head to toe. Zvar became a creature of the sea able to swim away from his mate... he could almost swear he heard her yelling from the beach, the desperation and fear causing him to only briefly falter as his strong strokes carried him away on the ocean currents.

Chapter 5

Zinnia grabbed the first piece of clothing her hands encountered, quickly pulling Zvar's t-shirt over her head. Her movements carried her off the bed as she tugged the soft cotton down over her rear.

She arrived on the edge of his deck just in time to spot him dive into the surf. Zinnia screamed his name and dug her feet into the beach as she tried to gain speed in the ever-shifting grains of sand with no success.

Zvar's head briefly rose above the water, allowing her to register that he had once again changed. No longer human in any way, she saw the creature of the sea he'd told her he could become. But, it didn't matter to her.

"Zvar! Please, come back." She continued to call for him for several long minutes but she never caught sight of his blue hair or his now fully scaled body.

He'd run from her. Why? Zinnia didn't understand what was going on. Hell, she knew she should be running for her life… away from Zvar not towards him. It made no sense, but she felt it in her heart and her gut that this was where she needed to be.

Not ready to go back inside or to give up on Zvar returning, Zinnia flopped to the sand and made herself comfortable. Her eyes roamed the waves as she leaned back on her hands and waited.

She'd always loved the water. Her parents had complained constantly, jokingly, that she must've been a fish in a former life because they'd had to pry her from the water. Bath time and swimming lessons always ended in tears when she was too little to understand why she couldn't do what she wanted to do.

Her love of the water was part of the reason she'd headed this direction when she saw the signs for the coast. And, why she'd stopped at the beach the previous night.

Wiggling her toes in the sand, she soaked up the heat that built up from the morning sun. The sound of the surf and the warmth of the sand lulled her into a light doze.

*

Cool water splashed against her legs, causing Zinnia to gasp in surprise as she opened her eyes to find a woman standing in front of her. The sun was lowering in the sky which caused the woman to appear as a shadow instead of flesh and blood.

"Hello," the lilting voice made Zinnia sway as she pushed herself up from the sand.

The new angle changed the lighting, allowing her to make out actual details about the woman... she was beautiful with long green-blue hair, which didn't appear weighed down by the water clinging to the strands.

A soft smile curved up the pale lips. The skin tone was difficult to determine as the reddish-colored rays of the sun bathed the stranger.

Deep down there was a feeling of kinship with this woman. Zinnia found no reasons for why, but she identified a familiar tug inside of herself. The sensation allowed her to relax and finally respond to the woman's greeting.

"Good evening. I'm sorry if I yelled. I must've fallen asleep." Zinnia glanced at the sky again.

Hours had passed since she'd followed Zvar out of his house. Thankfully, huddling inside of Zvar's large t-shirt had protected her body from unwanted sun damage. Her face was a bit warm, but not painful. Her hair must've been enough protection from the horrible sunburn she should have from being in the direct rays of the sun for so long.

"No worries, child. I'm sorry I woke you with the harsh cold of the sea." The voice reminded Zinnia of music... the tinkling of chimes.

She felt a pull, but not like the one Zvar caused her to experience, but similar all the same. Was this woman something more than human? Was she like Zvar? Could she help her find Zvar? The questions zinged through her mind until the woman laughed. The comparison to chimes becoming more apt with the sound of the stranger's laughter.

"I can tell you have questions... that you recognize some of what I am."

Zinnia nodded.

"How about we go inside?" The strange woman gestured to Zvar's home.

Cocking her head to see the woman's features more clearly, Zinnia didn't move from her current spot.

"I'm sorry, but I don't know you. Are you acquainted with the owner of the house?"

Chimes sounded as the woman walked past her. "Come, child, I'll explain once we're seated inside. I think you need a glass of water to keep from dehydrating."

Zinnia felt the tug again, but she fought to resist. She turned but did not move closer to Zvar's back deck where the woman was now climbing the few steps.

She must have realized Zinnia hadn't followed because the strange woman finally stopped and turned back to watch her intently.

"I won't be forced to do anything I'm not comfortable with," Zinnia stated as she crossed her arms. "As I said, I don't know you."

With the change in position, she made out more of the woman's features and was struck once again by her beauty. There was something about the eyes, which reminded her of Zvar and she wondered once again about a possible connection to the man she knew she had to find. They needed to determine what they meant to each other and whether or not that would mean Zinnia would remain here with him to explore it further.

"Child," the woman sighed. "I'd rather explain inside."

Fear crossed the woman's features but was quickly suppressed.

"Give me one good reason why," Zinnia demanded.

"Because you know my son and he needs you."

The stranger's eyes flashed with the same glow she'd seen in Zvar's eyes and scales rippled quickly across the skin before it turned smooth once again.

Zinnia searched inside herself. She felt that following this woman was the right thing to do and just like with Zvar, she could tell it wasn't the force of the woman's voice making her decide to do so.

By the time she made it inside, the woman was placing two large glasses of water on the table. Zinnia walked to the chair closest to her but braced herself against it rather than take a seat. She felt as if she could trust this woman but she still didn't know who she was. Zinnia may have gone from her normal everyday world into this fantasy world from the pages of some paranormal novel, but she still hoped some sanity remained in her life.

"Please, take a seat."

She hesitated to see if the compulsion from the woman's voice would force her to sit. She felt the power behind the beautiful sound but it appeared to have no influence over her — she took her seat and reached for the glass. Her many nights of watching cop shows had her pausing for a second before lifting the glass to her lips. *In for a penny, in for a pound, as the saying goes*, she thought as she gulped down the entire contents.

The woman reached out with a pitcher, refilling Zinnia's glass before finally taking the seat across from her. Zinnia's initial thirst was sated, and she slowly sipped at the cool liquid as she waited for the woman to speak.

"My name is Narcissca. Zvar is my son." She watched for Zinnia's reactions and continued when

Zinnia nodded for her to go on. "Zvar needs you. You are his mate. Sadly, it has been many years since he has returned to this stretch of beach... I haven't been able to be with him... my people... they won't accept him."

The woman sighed as she glanced out the sliding glass doors towards the sea.

"And, I can't be out of the water for long. I was forced to leave my son with the humans and hope they'd care for him. There was no way to know how his father's lineage would rise in him, but I knew he'd adapt to land as well as the deep depths of the ocean. His father wasn't a bad man, just controlled by his Unseelie Fae leaders. When he found me... we were destined mates... we completed each other, which meant he could control his need to steal someone's life force. I fed him all he needed. My mate wanted no one else. Vahn loved me and I him... we both loved the child we created."

Zinnia saw love and pain mirrored in the deep blue eyes.

"We conceived Zvar our first night together, when we claimed each other. Finding my destined mate made me happy beyond words and Vahn felt the same. He bought a house along this beach — this house in fact — it allowed us to spend our nights in his bed and our days on the ocean. He became a fisherman in order for us to never be far apart. Being mated allowed me to spend more time on land, but not all of my time. I still had to return to the water. We both left our people behind because neither race would accept us. When it got closer to time for me to give birth, I had to spend more time in the water. There's a cave hidden below the waves I stayed in while still being close to the beach. It was during one such time when Vahn's people tracked him down. I sensed his fear and swam as fast as I could, but I only arrived in time to witness them disappear with my unconscious mate in their arms. Without Vahn, I feared for our child. Even though it was the hardest thing I've ever had to do, I swaddled our son in a blanket and left him in a basket on a neighbors porch. I kept watch until he was discovered. Since then… I've only been able to search for information, never able to join him. A friend, Clyde, mentored Zvar for me. Clyde providing me second-hand details about my son was the closest I've ever been able to be to Zvar. My people captured me too, you see… my father married me to a merman he felt was worthy. But, he's not my mate and nothing they do can force a bond between us."

Tears fell from Zvar's mother's eyes as she finished her story.

"I'm so sorry for your loss. Is Zvar's father dead?" Zinnia wasn't sure why she asked, but a need to know pushed her and forced the words forth.

"I can't say for sure. The bond isn't broken like it would be if he was… it's just sort of ends… I think they took him to the Fae realm. Our bond can't reach between the realms and he wouldn't be able to feed on the energy he'd need to survive. I'm not sure how he could still be alive after all of these years."

Zinnia reached out her hand and placed it over Narcissca's.

"Why are you here now?"

"Clyde got word to me. He feared Zvar had finally lost his battle with his Unseelie side. I was at the beach watching for him when he carried you home. I sensed the connection and recognized you as his salvation. But, then, I saw him rush away this morning. I wasn't sure what to do, but when the coast was clear, I came to shore... to enlist your help. My son needs you."

"Narcissca, my name is Zinnia. I would do anything for Zvar."

"Are you sure? You must be positive before I can ask of you what I must."

"Yes. I don't know how I know or how it happened so quickly, but I love him. He is *mine*."

Narcissca's face lit up with her smile as she grasped Zinnia's hands. "I knew you were the one. Now we pull forth your inner mermaid, and you can follow Zvar and bring him back."

"What?" Zinnia squeaked.

"Yes, Zinnia, in your ancestry you have Merfolk. You've inherited enough to provide us with what we need."

"Um, no. I'm one hundred percent human. Even Zvar mentioned that fact. What makes you think I have something that even he didn't sense?"

"Because I'm one hundred percent mermaid and have been taught our ways my whole life. You can feel the tug towards me, can't you? Not as strong as the one to Zvar, but it's there isn't it?"

Zinnia contemplated the situation for some minutes. She had noticed it but attributed it to the compulsion in the two paranormal creatures voices.

Could it really be what Narcissca was saying? Was she really part mermaid?

"But, how? And, if your people wouldn't accept Zvar before, how would they accept me or him now? I don't want to be confined to the ocean for the rest of my life. I've always loved the water, but not enough to give up my... human life."

"Not even for Zvar?"

Zinnia's mouth dropped open, and she gaped at Narcissca. She wanted to deny it, to say not even for Zvar, but the truth was she would give her life for him. She already knew the man, the Fae-Merfolk hybrid, had weaseled his way into her heart. Yes, she loved him — she loved the same man who had run from her just that morning.

"But, why did he run?" she mumbled under her breath.

"Because he's scared and doesn't think he's good enough for you," Narcissca responded.

"What do I need to do?" Zinnia was terrified but determined.

"First, we need to go into the ocean, then, I sing."

Chapter 6

*N*arcissca led Zinnia out into the ocean until they were chest deep before stopping and turning to her.

"I've only seen this done once, it appeared to be painful... but, you must hang on and not let go of your desire to become more."

"So, I just picture myself as a mermaid while you sing?"

"Basically, yes. I need you to hold on to my arms. It's very important that you don't let go. No matter what, hold on to me."

Zinnia gulped down her fear and nodded to Narcissca. She was as prepared as she could be for what was about to happen. Reaching out she grabbed onto Narcissca as instructed while closing her eyes. An image easily arose in her mind's eye. She hadn't thought up the picture; it was conjured by her desire to join Zvar below the ocean waves. Her desire to bring him home.

Pain sliced through her arms and legs as she fought to keep hold of Zvar's mother. Water lapped at her body.

Soon the pain receded. Her vision of herself as a mermaid returned, and she clung to the vision as strongly as she held on to Narcissca's arms. Chimes seeped into her awareness, they didn't wake her but simply guided her deeper into her vision.

The vision showed her swimming quickly through the water with the sun glinting off of her copper scales. She loved the warmth of the sun's rays as she crested the waves. The contrast of the warmth after the coolness made her heart want to burst with joy. Her hair had darkened until it became coal black, but it remained the same length as it was in her human form. Happiness filled her as she listened to the song of the ocean. It called to her. It cradled her close in its cool arms.

"Zinnia, open your eyes."

Narcissca's voice shocked her awake. She couldn't remember the siren's song or the passage of time. She just knew it had been hours since she'd entered the water. Almost afraid the magic hadn't worked, Zinnia opened her eyes to the beauty that lived under the surface of the ocean. Swiveling her head she felt panic seep in and squeeze her lungs. *She couldn't breathe water, she needed oxygen.*

"Calm, Zinnia. You are fine. Concentrate on breathing, you'll feel the water flowing through your gills." She felt Narcissca lightly touch a spot on either side of her throat.

That was when she felt the sensation of water moving in and out of her through those spots on her neck. Her body instinctively processed the water, removing the much-needed oxygen while expelling the rest.

She *was* breathing underwater! It had worked. Zinnia's gaze lowered to her hands, which now had webs connecting the fingers and the copper scales from her vision covered her skin. She grinned up at Narcissca.

"Where do we go from here?" she asked.

Narcissca smiled. "I knew you were the one."

She stroked Zinnia's hair back from her face and smiled.

"I will lead you to the cave where he normally goes. You must go in alone. I'm afraid, I would only make things worse."

Once again, Zinnia was hit by the sadness and loss vibrating from Narcissca every time she spoke of her son or her mate. The woman had lost everything.

She felt a need to not only help Zvar see the truth of who he was, but also a need to repair the family that had never had a chance to be together.

"Then, let's go."

*

Narcissca led Zinnia to the mouth of a cave. If it wasn't for her need for Zvar causing her body to ache, Zinnia would have rejoiced at her new ability to swim and breath under the water. Her childhood love of the water finally made sense.

The two women spoke as they traveled, but Narcissca couldn't say how far back in her ancestry Zinnia's mermaid ancestor was located. The mermaid insisted she knew nothing more… simply, calling Zinnia special. That was the word the siren had used, *special*. She wasn't sure if she should be afraid or excited, but Narcissca had refused to enlighten her on what she meant. Zvar's mother had insisted her son's needs came first, then, if both he and Zinnia wanted to find out more about their heritage, she'd be willing to teach them.

Zinnia floated next to Zvar's mother, both staring into the gaping maw of the cave. Fear wavered on the edges of her brain, but she shoved it down further. There was no going back for her now — she was a mermaid with a mate that needed her.

The older mermaid turned to her with an intent look. She didn't speak just gazed at Zinnia causing a shiver to race up the newly turned mermaid's spine.

"What is wrong, Narcissca?"

"Nothing." She shook her head while turning her gaze back to the cave. "Your bravery amazes me... you are braver than I ever was. I let my family keep me away from my son... now he thinks I abandoned him, that his father and I didn't love him."

"You said you couldn't leave the ocean. What else could you have done?" Zinnia had always been empathic towards others.

It was natural for her to reach out to place her hand on the other female's arm.

Narcissca's eyes focused on Zinnia's hand. Finding it strange, Zinnia glanced down to see why the mermaid had such a strange expression. What she discovered had her jerking her hand back and holding it to her chest.

Zinnia's hand glowed.

Narcissca quickly gripped Zinnia's hands in her own.

"Do not fear it. You are *special*."

"What the fuck does that mean?" Zinnia wasn't one to curse, but her fear had risen and overpowered her resolve to stay calm.

The siren sighed. "I wanted to wait until you were ready, until you were both ready," she mumbled. "Zinnia, you are a healer, an empath. It is a rare gift in the Merfolk. Your dark hair and copper scales identify you as a strong healer. We haven't had one born in centuries."

"But, why would you not want to tell me?"

"Because my people wouldn't care about you being my son's mate. They would force you to mate with someone of their choosing, then take your children away from you. They would essentially make you into a broodmare to create the healer's our race no longer have."

Zinnia gaped at the woman. *What the hell is wrong with these people?* She wondered. Then, realized, they weren't people, they were paranormal creatures that had a different belief system than the human one Zinnia was raised with.

"Don't worry, child, I won't let them have you. I will do what I was too afraid to do before... I will protect my son, he needs you, Zinnia, which means I must protect you as well — you're my daughter now. Go... get your mate."

The mermaid gave her a reassuring smile as she shoved her towards the cave.

Zinnia drifted slowly towards the mouth of the cave, but she still arrived at the entrance faster than she desired. Glancing over her shoulder she laughed out loud as Narcissca gave her a huge smile and two-thumbs-up. It was the most unexpected vision, a siren under the ocean sending her off like a best friend would when a girl planned to flirt with a crush. Sadly, she had a hunch Zvar wouldn't make this situation as easy.

Chapter 7

*Z*var floated in the deepest area of the cave near his home. It was a place for him to hide away from the real world that existed above the waves. It was also a place where his mate couldn't tempt him. He was not worthy of her and refused to tie her to him for eternity. With his Fae-Siren blood, his life would last a very long time, possibly, forever. Most thought the Fae to be immortal, which meant there was a good chance he could be as well.

Warm currents intermixed with the cooler ones, which soothed his aching soul. The water was always a balm on his fractured psyche. The beast couldn't control him here, not when he was closer to his mother's side of his family.

As he reclined in the water, letting it buoy his body, fire burned through his veins. Smells were different here, but he'd almost swear the water carried his sweet Zinnia to him. But, it couldn't be true, she was safe up in his home. Away from him and the danger he posed to her.

His memories simply played tricks on him.

A disturbance in the water alerted him he was no longer alone. He quickly swam behind a large boulder which shielded him from view. Someone was in his cave.

Clyde had always told him to be extremely careful in the ocean, warning him the Merfolk would not accept him. In fact, Clyde had told him there was a death warrant for anyone with mixed blood like himself. It wasn't his or any other child's fault they were born a hybrid, but it didn't matter to the Merfolk, to them anyone who diluted their bloodlines was considered a criminal deserving to die. In Zvar's opinion, only someone evil would want to punish an innocent. Granted, Zvar wouldn't place himself in the innocent category any longer, but as a child, he had been. He might not have been in control of his powers, but he'd also had no idea about his lineage and the changes occurring in him. Hell, if he'd been able to be with one or both of his parents, surely he would've been raised understanding the monster inside and how to control it. He believed that idea with all of his heart, which was why he'd always wondered why his mother and father abandoned him.

Shaking off the past, Zvar focused on the present.

A glow appeared in the passage leading to the opened area where he'd been resting. *Damn it*, he berated himself. He couldn't afford to lose focus.

The truth… Zvar might think of himself as a monster, but he wasn't ready to die. A vision of Zinnia flashed into his mind but he pushed it away… his mate did not need him. He needed to remember she would be better off without him in her life. His sweet flower was better off without him stealing her inner light.

As the seconds ticked by, the glow solidified into the eyes of a mermaid. The only one he had ever seen in person and she was devastatingly gorgeous. He felt his body react to her as he filled with lust. Hatred seeped into his heart — how could he allow himself to even think of someone else in that way with his mate only a short swim away on land. Zvar dug his fingers into his palm, but nothing was dampening his desire. There was something about this mermaid. She called to him, like...

It didn't matter, Zinnia was his fated mate and he would not forsake her for another. Even if he wasn't good enough for her, he wouldn't replace her. He would be alone for the rest of his long — or maybe short — life. So, he fought the pull of the female with everything he had. No one would affect him this way except for his sweet mate. Zvar may not want to claim her — for her own good — but he wanted no one else either.

"Zvar?" The familiar voice quivered as the mermaid wrapped her arms around herself. "Damn it, where the hell are you?"

Her bottom lip poked out as she flipped her shoulder-length hair, the dark strands brought to mind similar hair fanned out on his sheets.

"Zinnia?" he called as he pushed out from behind the boulder.

And, his mate screamed. Zvar sped to her side, cradling her in his arms before she could do anything to harm herself. Her eyes lay closed.

He'd caused her to faint... again.

A commotion in the tunnel caused him to push through the water, barricading himself and Zinnia behind the boulder he'd only recently left. With Zinnia out of harm's way, he stepped out to brace for whatever was coming for him and his mate. He would take care of the intruder, then he'd figure out how his human mate had grown scales and learned to breathe underwater.

A female siren swam out of the narrow passage while frantically searching around. When her eyes landed on Zvar, her hand immediately covered her mouth. He saw tears welling at the corners of her eyes before the current carried them away. Something about the woman called to him. She was familiar, but he had never met a mermaid face-to-face, so how could she be familiar? Unless...

"Zinnia, is she okay? I heard her scream." The voice was low, quivering with uncertainty.

"Who are you?" he asked.

"Zinnia?" she called.

After her initial reaction, the woman kept her gaze focused anywhere, but on Zvar himself. But, he wouldn't tell her anything about his mate unless she answered him first.

"Who are you?" he insisted.

Her shoulders slumped inward, and she appeared to shrink in on herself.

"I'm your mother, Zvar. Now, please tell me Zinnia's safe?"

He gaped at her. He'd thought she might be a relative, but not the mother who had abandoned him.

"Leave," he roared without a conscious decision to do so.

His emotions controlled him.

"I will, if that is what you want, as soon as I see that Zinnia is not harmed."

"You have no rights here. You lost those when you left me up there." His hand jabbed up towards the beach.

He wouldn't have thought it possible, but the siren collapsed even further into herself.

"You are right. I just... I... please make sure Zinnia is okay."

With those words, she turned to leave. His heart fractured. She'd leave him so easily again? True, he'd told her to leave, but shouldn't she fight for her own son?

"Wait." Zinnia groaned from behind him. "Narcissca, don't go." She gripped the rock to pull herself forward.

Zvar's eyes moved back and forth between the two women. The one that had abandoned him faced the one he had abandoned. The sadness on Zinnia's face slapped him like a physical thing. He was no better than what he accused his parents of since he was old enough to realize he'd been left alone in a strange world. A world in which he never fit, even before he'd learned what he was.

"Mother..." he choked on the word but forced himself to continue. "Wait."

Zinnia gave him a small smile of encouragement as the mermaid turned to face him again.

"Just tell me, why?"

"It's a long story, but essentially... your father's people captured him and I was left alone. I feared I couldn't protect you from my people... I believed they couldn't find you as long as you lived on land as a human. Leaving you was the hardest thing I ever had to do."

Tears flowed quickly from the corners of her eyes, causing streams in the water before the tears dissipated into the surrounding ocean.

Zinnia rushed forward and wrapped the other woman in her arms. The second they made contact, both of them glowed. Zvar stood in shock as he saw his mate comfort his mother. His female soothed the other mermaid, helping her to return to the confident woman he had seen for a few minutes as she swam to his mate's rescue.

His woman looked up from his mother and smiled.

"She is telling you the truth, Zvar."

"I know."

Zinnia broke out in laughter. His mother soon joined her.

"It wouldn't hurt you to use more than two words at one time, Zvar." His mate continued to chuckle as the glow receded and she led his mother forward. "Zvar, this is Narcissca, she is your mother. She loves you very much."

Gazing into Zinnia's eyes, Zvar knew one thing, he loved this woman and he would do anything she asked. Obviously, she wanted him to know his own mother.

"Mother," he nodded in greeting causing the woman to smile.

"Zinnia, I should leave. This is about you and Zvar."

Zinnia protested until his mother stopped his mate with a finger laid on her lips.

"Child, I won't be far. I told you I'd be here for the both of you if that was what you decided. Now, take care of my son. Talk to him."

The siren laid a kiss on Zinnia's cheek, gave him a smile, then swam away. His head throbbed as it struggled to process everything. How? Why? What? All of the typical questions zoomed through him. But, then Zinnia turned to him and floated close enough to wrap her arms around his waist.

"Now, Zvar, I know there is a lot to discuss, but let's start with... Why did you run from me? Don't you want me?"

His heart constricted at the fear and heartbreak in those last words. He only had one answer for his female.

Zvar's lips slammed down on Zinnia's. He consumed her mouth with his own until her lips were swollen from his kisses. Licking and probing until she allowed him inside, he drowned on the flavor of his mate. Zvar could live on her kisses alone for eternity. He had been the largest of fools for running from her. A glow engulfed them but he didn't care. His hands stroked down her sides until he caressed between her legs. She was ready for him and he was more than ready for her.

In their mermaid forms their bodies were still humanoid and his cock rose from the protective scales. This time, he would claim his woman. She came for him, it had to mean she wanted him in return. How could he deny her anything she wanted? He couldn't, even if it meant giving himself.

"Will you be my mate, Zinnia?"

"Yes," she groaned as he latched onto one of her gorgeous nipples.

The texture of her skin, so different from when she was human...

"Wait." He pushed away to hold her at arm's length.

His mate moaned and pouted up at him.

"What?"

"How can you be here? You're human."

She laughed. "Ah, that. Well,... um... I wasn't one hundred percent human, more like ninety-five point three percent human."

He shook his head trying to figure out what she was trying to tell him.

"Your mom sensed my small percentage. She offered the magic for me to grown scales and go after you, so here I am in the scales." She grinned up at him while waiting for his response.

"You... you..." He pulled her close, laying kisses along her jaw and lips. "You're amazing."

"Now, can you make me yours, Zvar? I think I waited long enough."

He laughed then drowned himself in his mate. How could he ever think of leaving her?

Chapter 8

*Z*var woke in his mate's arms. He had claimed her in the cavern below the ocean, then he'd carried her from the water and into his home where he had claimed her again.

Her transformation from mermaid to human was something to behold. His mate was beautiful in either form. But, watching it happen had plagued him with many questions. Not able to sleep after Zinnia had fallen asleep, he rose from the bed and pulled on a pair of jeans. He wandered outside to find his mother sitting on the porch steps.

"I'm sorry," she whispered on the wind.

With a sigh, Zvar sat beside the woman. She was a complete stranger, yet she wasn't. The breeze blew in from the ocean, picking up the sand as it moved inland. He observed the grains catch the light of the moon as they danced in the air.

"I can leave if that is what you want," his mother offered.

"No… I have questions."

"Okay then, go ahead."

Zvar knew what he wanted to ask but fear strangled his words. So, with a deep breath, he asked another pressing question.

"How did Zinnia become a mermaid?"

"Ah, yes… magic brought out DNA she already possessed."

"Will it hurt her? Can it be reversed? Will she be in danger? Can she stay on land?"

His mother let out a low chuckle as she placed a hand on his arm to stop him. Zvar shook with the first contact he ever truly remembered having with this female. As the siren smiled up at him, long forgotten memories surfaced. Memories of her smile. He remembered her holding him as an infant and even heard the song she used to sing him to sleep with. But, how? He was so small when he was left on a doorstep on this very beach.

"Zvar?"

His gaze snapped up from where they had focused on her fingers laying against the skin of his arm.

"Your mate is safe. She will need to practice keeping her mermaid side hidden when necessary; otherwise, she can live as she was living before. Oh, she will need to visit the ocean a few times a year. Something about the salty water of the Earth's oceans soothes the Merfolk. She will have to be careful…"

"Careful of what?"

"Of the Merfolk. They will want to take her from you. She is precious… we have not seen one such as her in an extremely long time."

"No one will take my mate from me," he growled as scales slid over his skin.

His hair lengthened and tickled the skin of his neck as the breeze picked up.

"Of course not, my son."

He swung his gaze back to his mother's face. He had been staring out to the sea, searching for attackers, when he heard those words with the love they carried.

"I... I... I'm not..."

"Oh..." Narcissca's hand rose to her mouth as if to keep herself from saying something more, but she quickly dropped it to continue. "I just... Zvar, you are my son. Whether or not you want to consider me your mother is up to you, but you will always be my son. I'll always regret the time we were separated. Clyde told me how difficult the humans were, but... but, at least you're still alive."

"Clyde? What... Wait! What do you mean still alive?"

A weary sigh escaped, but his mother only took a minute to gather her thoughts.

"To be blunt, paranormal beings are elitist and racist. The Unseelie Fae kidnapped your father and without him, I couldn't protect you from the Merfolk. They'd want to kill you for simply not being a hundred percent merman."

Zvar's shoulders sagged as he realized he'd always be an outcast and now, so would his mate. Zinnia wasn't a hundred percent mermaid, which meant she'd be in danger as well.

"Zinnia, on the other hand, they would covet her for what she is."

"Wait... what is she?"

"Your mate is a healer. If they learn of her, they will want her... they'd want to use her for breeding. To breed more like her."

Zvar jumped to his feet as he paced. His mind whirled with what little he'd learned. He struggled with the memories and emotions of the small boy who always felt abandoned. But, the man who he'd become wanted to mend the rift between his past and present. Zvar didn't want to act stupidly and lose his mother again. If at all possible, he would never be parted from his family again. Zinnia and his mother were his family. He would protect them with his life.

His decision made, Zvar turned on his heel and strode to his mother. She struggled to her feet while worry played out in the lines of her face and the curve of her shoulders. Without a word, he pulled her into his embrace and hugged the woman who'd given him life. Her body heaved as her tears streamed down her face, coating his skin.

"I didn't think you would want me?"

"You are my mother. I've decided the past should be left in the past. However, I want to understand the reason, but I refuse to lose a member of my family over something that happened a long time ago. You are here now and Zinnia will need you. I need you."

Holding her out at arm's length he stared into eyes much like his own. His mother reached up and slid her fingers over his jaw.

"You look so much like your father." Zvar winced as his mother gripped his face in her small hands. "Your father was a good male. He fought his Unseelie needs until he found me and I could feed him. Our family was all he wanted in this world. We made a life here in this house until they snatched him away."

"This was your house?" The pieces clicked into place.

Zvar now knew why Clyde talked him into renting this home. He'd also learned that his mother and Clyde knew each other from her earlier slip. It was obvious she'd been caring for her son. From afar, true, but she'd still been there.

"Yes." She grinned. "Still is actually."

"Ah... well, landlord, I need to speak to you about the lack of closet space..." They both broke out laughing and the tension seeped away.

"Well, well, well. Isn't this a lovely sight?" Zinnia yawned as she smiled at him and his mother.

Zvar was at her side, pulling her into his arms, before he had even finished the thought. Their lips smashed together, and they explored each other's mouths without thought of anything happening around them.

"Ahem. I'm just going to go for a dip. I'll return... let's say in a few hours."

Zvar was lost in his mate's scent and taste. All he could do was wave his mother away as he scooped Zinnia into his embrace to return her to their bedroom.

Epilogue

Zinnia stood on her new back deck, smiling at the view in front of her. A year had passed since she'd stopped at the beach in Rodanthe, North Carolina and she couldn't be happier with the direction of her life.

The changes weren't easy for any of them but Zvar, his mother, and Zinnia were building a family. They'd suffered both ups and downs as Zvar learned more about his powers while Zinnia learned her own.

Now, they'd put down roots in the Midwest. The location was the complete opposite of where their story began but no less beautiful.

Her and Zvar had discovered the racism against hybrids was worse than anything they'd imagined. As a healer — *God, I love being a healer,* she thought — those in need drew her to them and they'd soon collected quite the following. It only made sense to gather everyone in a stronghold of some sort.

So, they'd bought this land along with Zvar's mother, creating a paranormal safe house for hybrid children and adults. Even Narcissca was now living with them full time.

With the wealth Zvar's mother gifted them for their mating, they'd had more than enough to purchase this piece of land and all that surrounded it for at least twenty-five miles. The past year had been spent building and several cottages surrounded two ponds. The siren had worked with other magical beings to create an ocean environment in one of the ponds while keeping the other as fresh water. They'd actually used magic to create several different habitat regions. Zinnia wished for all the hybrids to be comfortable and have everything they needed, and her family had worked tirelessly to create a hybrid sanctuary.

The most important part of their new home, though, were the wards protecting them all from the paranormal world that didn't want to accept them. Narcissca along with a few Fae-Witch hybrids worked together to create a magical barrier strong enough to keep any race at bay. The barrier only allowed humans and paranormals who meant no harm and those seeking refuge to enter. Anyone who didn't need safe shelter or have business with those within the barrier would be diverted. Thus, protecting the sanctuary's anonymity.

A year ago, she was searching for a direction, a purpose and Fate saw to it that she got exactly what she needed. Now, she was a Human-Mermaid hybrid with the power to heal others. She also had a wonderful mate who made her deliriously happy.

"What has brought this blush to your cheeks, my sweet?" Zvar wrapped his arms around her from behind while laying soft kisses on her exposed neck.

"Nothing..." Her mate tensed, he always recognized when she was lying. "Fine, I was thinking about this morning before I got out of bed."

Zvar groaned, but his real response pressed into her backside.

"Don't get any ideas, we have supplies coming that need to be unloaded. Besides, I have to work with the Gargoyle-Wolf twins. I'm hoping to coax them into shifting today."

"I hate being responsible," her mate grumbled. "But, it would be nice to speak to them and find out if there are more like them. Besides, they sort of creep me out. I mean, I keep finding them perched on the roof staring at me."

Zinnia smacked his arm and laughed as he pulled her into his embrace.

"I love you, Zinnia. You are my strength. You give me purpose. Hell, you saved me, woman."

"I love you too, Zvar. You are my everything." With her last word, Zinnia went up on tiptoe and wrapped her arms around Zvar's neck.

A brush of her lips was all it took for him to push his tongue into her mouth and take over the kiss. When Zvar kissed her, it was more like he consumed her. Zinnia felt the glow wrap around them as she shared her life force with him. Her soul was now whole and she had more than enough strength within her to share with her mate.

*J*osette Reuel spent many years in the corporate world writing stuffy computer software manuals, until one day a shape-shifting dragon kidnapped her and dragged her off to be his destined mate... as the words flowed onto the page, she realized that it was time to fulfill her lifelong dream of becoming a published author.

An avid reader from her earliest memories, Josette enjoys many genres; however, her current passion is anything Romance. Her love of Fantasy and the Paranormal tends to come out in all of her writing with strong alpha heroes, each with a little something extra.

Josette writes paranormal romance of varying degrees of heat. She believes in LOVE in all of its forms and doesn't discriminate or sensor her muse. If you enjoy reading a love story, if you enjoy paranormal creatures, alpha males, and the heroes/heroines that change their lives, then she's positive you'll enjoy the worlds she creates on the page.

Connect With Me Online

Twitter: https://twitter.com/JosetteReuel
Facebook:
    https://www.facebook.com/josette.reuel
    https://www.facebook.com/JosetteReuelAuthor
    https://www.facebook.com/groups/dasreachwarriors
Google+: https://plus.google.com/+JosetteReuel
Pinterest: http://www.pinterest.com/josettereuel/
Instagram: https://www.instagram.com/josettereuel/
Goodreads: https://www.goodreads.com/evanlea
BookBub: https://www.bookbub.com/authors/josette-reuel

Booksprout: https://booksprout.co/author/1463/josette-reuel

Web site: http://JosetteReuel.weebly.com

Authorgraph: https://www.authorgraph.com/authors/JosetteReuel

Books By Josette Reuel

Dásreach Council Novels

Book 1: Finding the Dragon

Book 2: Accepting the Bear

Book 3: Releasing the Panther

Book 3.5: A Second Life As A Bear

Book 4: Loving a Bear and Wolf (TBA)

Draghue Dragon Series

1.0: Love Burns

Gwar'Arth of Karhu Ridge Series

1.0: Subtle Magic

2.0: Creative Magic

Hybrid Home Series

1.0: Fated Summer

Holiday Pack Series

Wolves for the Holiday 1.1

Wolves for the Holiday 1.2

Wolves for the Holiday 1.3

Scaredy Cat Series

1.0: Caught By Love (Released in the "A Guide to | Claiming a Scaredy Cat" anthology April 2018)

Spencer's Helpline Series

1.0: Shift or Treat

2.0 Mistletoe Magic

Valentine's Voodoo Series

1.0: Swan Dive

2.0: Swan's Grace

3.0: Swan Song

Did You Enjoy This Book?

If you enjoyed reading this book, I appreciate your help in letting other readers enjoy it, too.

Recommend it. Help others find this book by recommending it to friends, readers groups, and discussion boards.

Review it. Tell others about why you liked this book by reviewing it at your retailer, Goodreads, and/or your blog. Reader reviews help authors continue to be valued by retailers and help new readers make decisions when choosing books. I appreciate all feedback and look forward to seeing your review.

Made in the USA
Middletown, DE
24 April 2019